ARE THE DINOSAURS DEAD, DAD?

Julie Middleton

illustrated by Russell Ayto

PICTURE CORGI

For Sam, Frankie and Harley J.M.

For Alyx, Greta, Emilio and Loveday –
I'm not extinct, just busy! R.A.

ARE THE DINOSAURS DEAD, DAD?
A PICTURE CORGI BOOK
978 0 552 563666
Published in Great Britain by
Picture Corgi, an imprint of
Random House Children's Publishers UK
A Random House Group Company
This edition published 2012
1 3 5 7 9 10 8 6 4 2

RANDOM HOUSE CHILDREN'S
PUBLISHERS UK, 61–63 Uxbridge Road,
London W5 5SA
www.**kidsatrandomhouse**.co.uk
www.**randomhouse**.co.uk
Addresses for companies
within The Random House
Group Limited can be found at:
www.randomhouse.
co.uk/offices.htm
THE RANDOM HOUSE GROUP
Limited Reg. No. 954009
A CIP catalogue record
for this book is available
from the British Library.
Printed in China

"Are the dinosaurs dead, Dad?"
asked Dave.

"Dead?" Dad said.
"Yes, the dinosaurs are dead."

"Oh!"
said Dave.

Number of Dinosaurs
Years Ago (in millions)
0

"Now, this handsome fella," explained Dad, "is the **Ankylosaurus**. Look at the fabulous armour plating and bony eyelids."

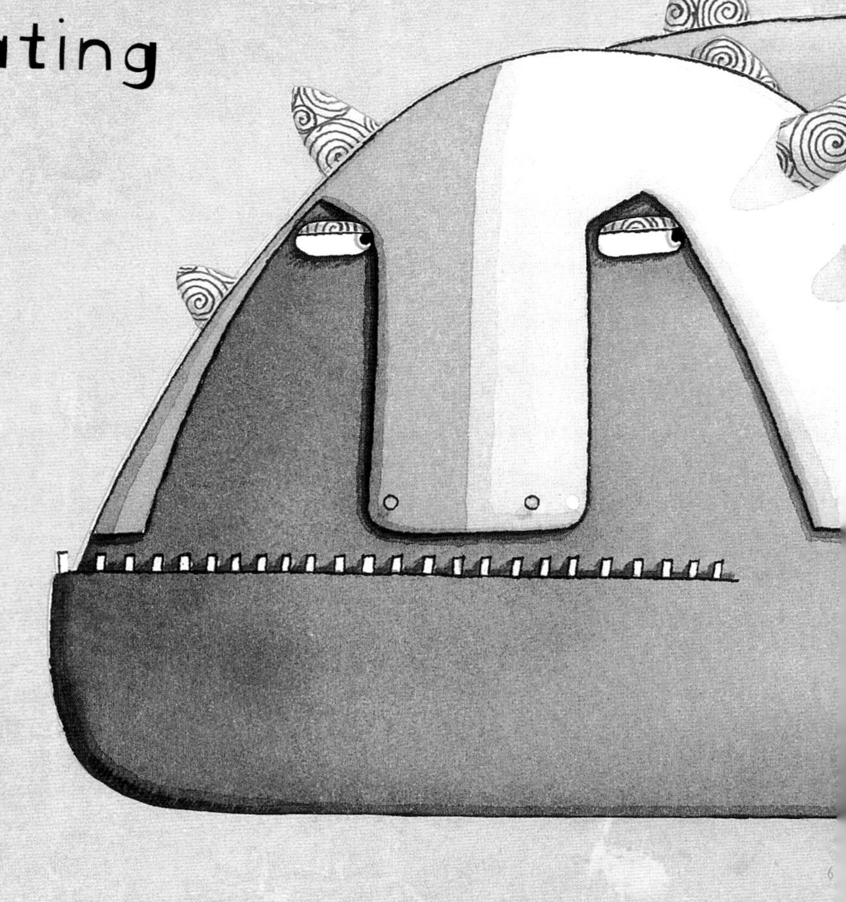

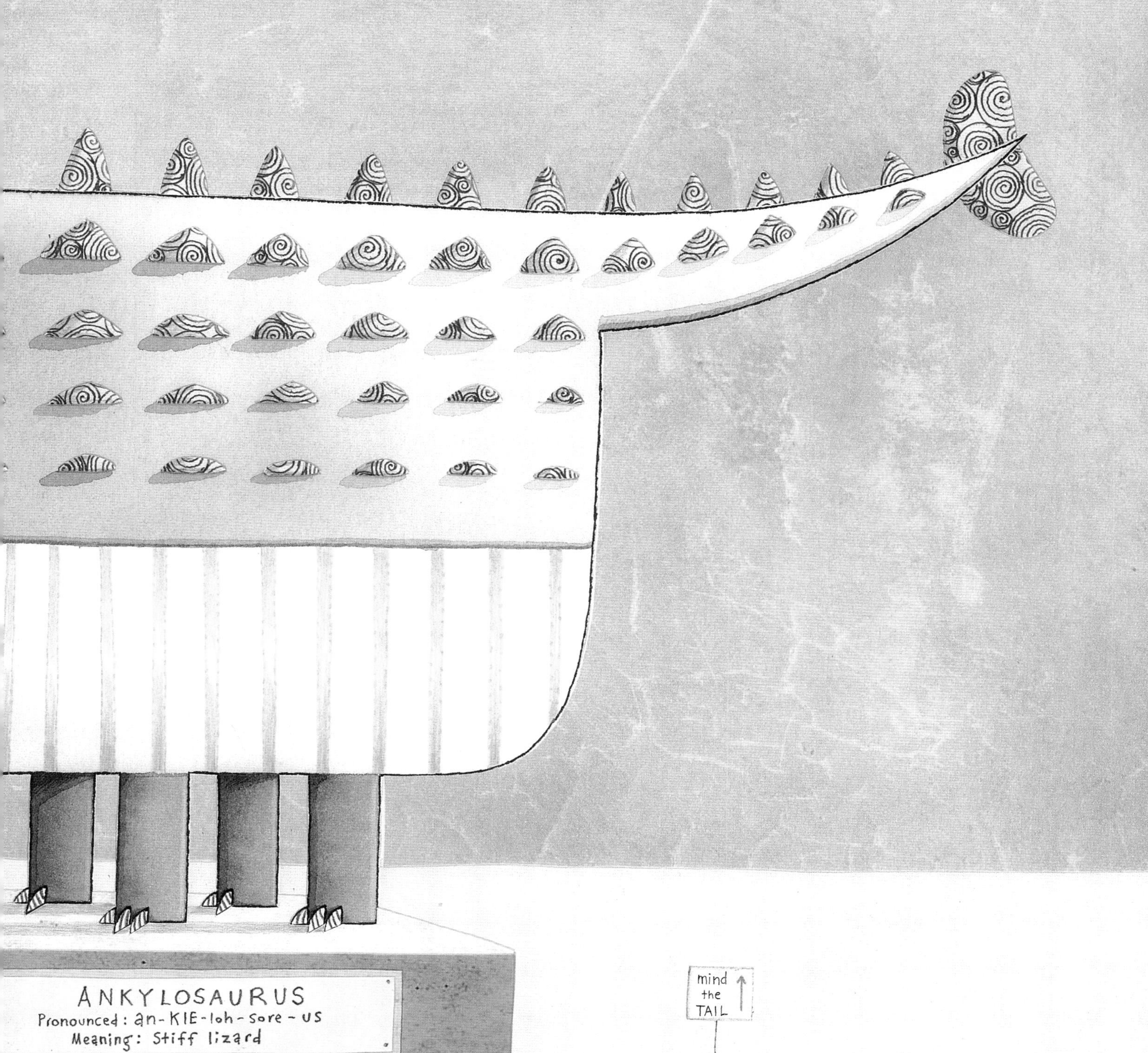
ANKYLOSAURUS
Pronounced: an-KIE-loh-sore-us
Meaning: Stiff lizard
mind the TAIL

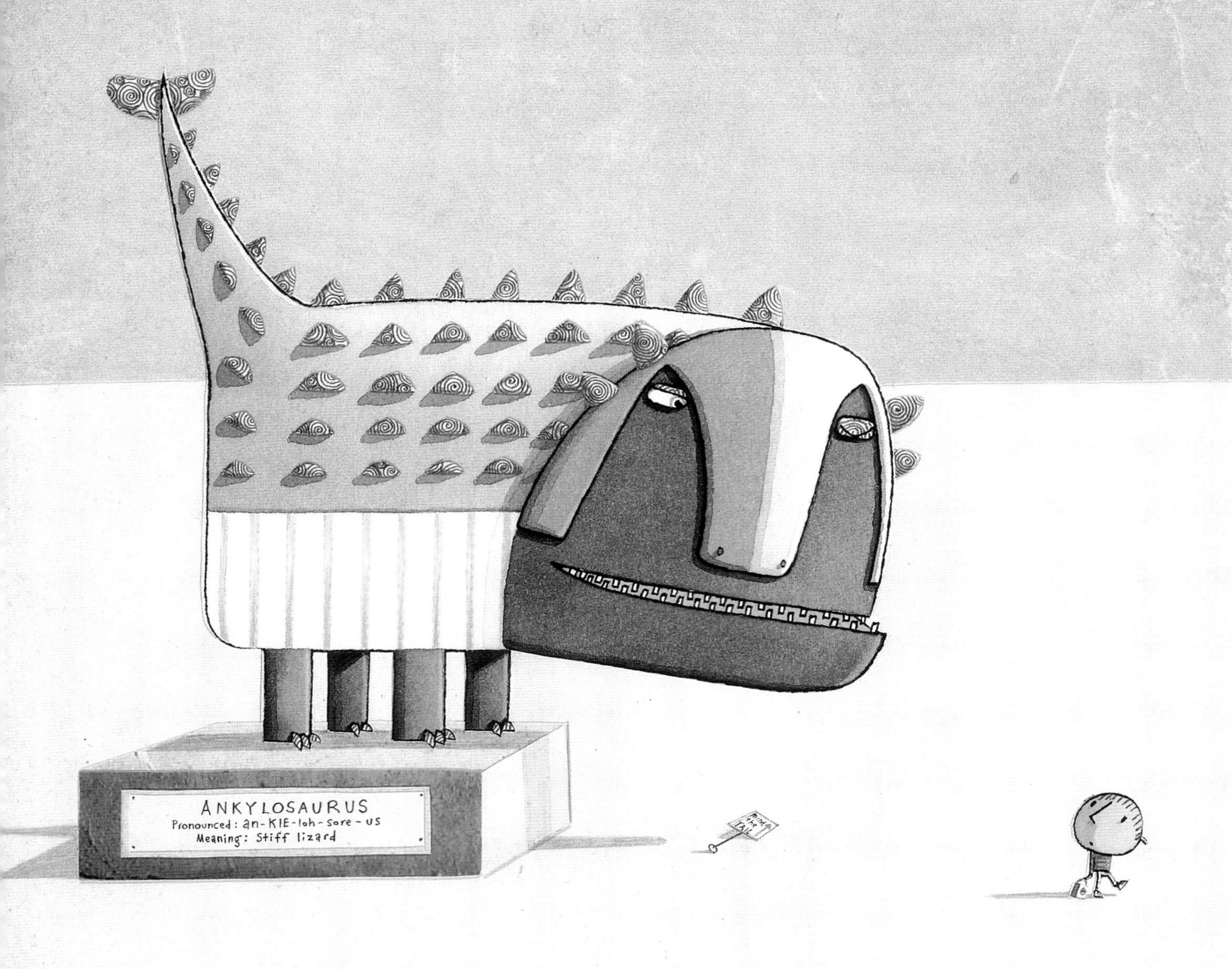

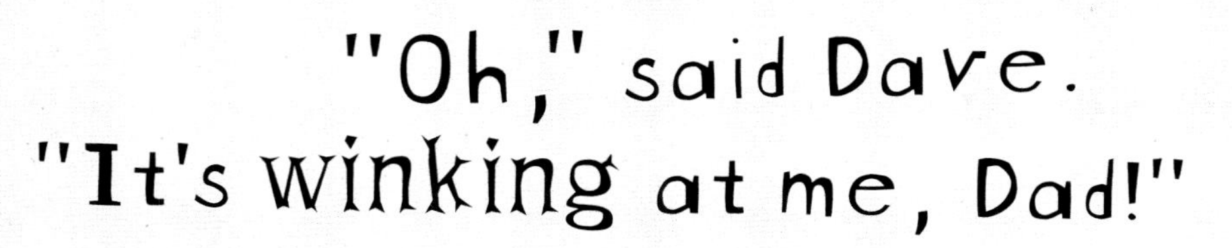

"Oh," said Dave.
"It's winking at me, Dad!"

"Ankylosaurus
don't wink, Dave,"
said Dad,
"it's just your
imagination."

"You see, Dave," said Dad, knowledgeably, "that dinosaur there is the **Deinocheirus**. It has the longest arms of all the dinosaurs."

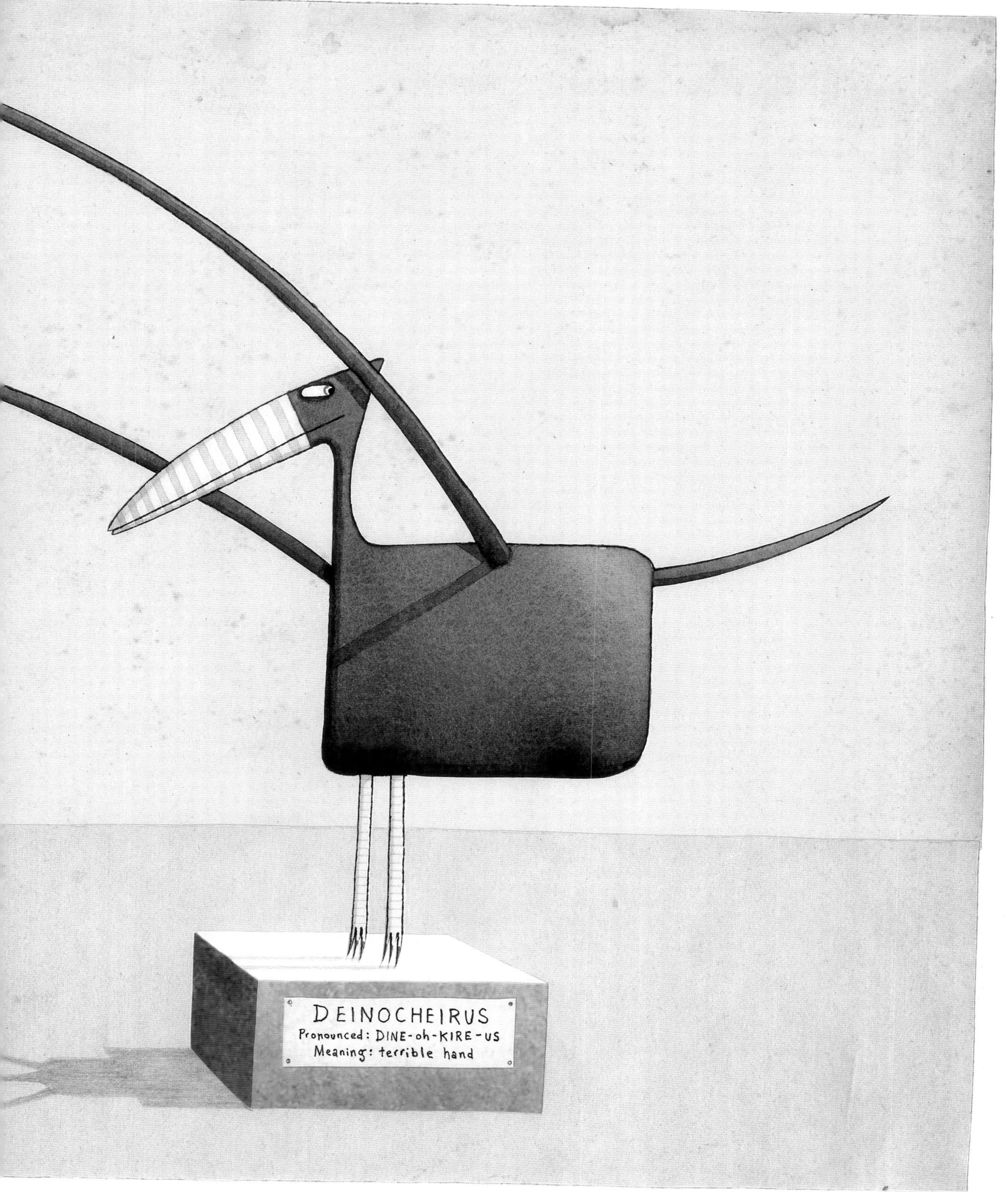
DEINOCHEIRUS
Pronounced: DINE-oh-KIRE-US
Meaning: terrible hand

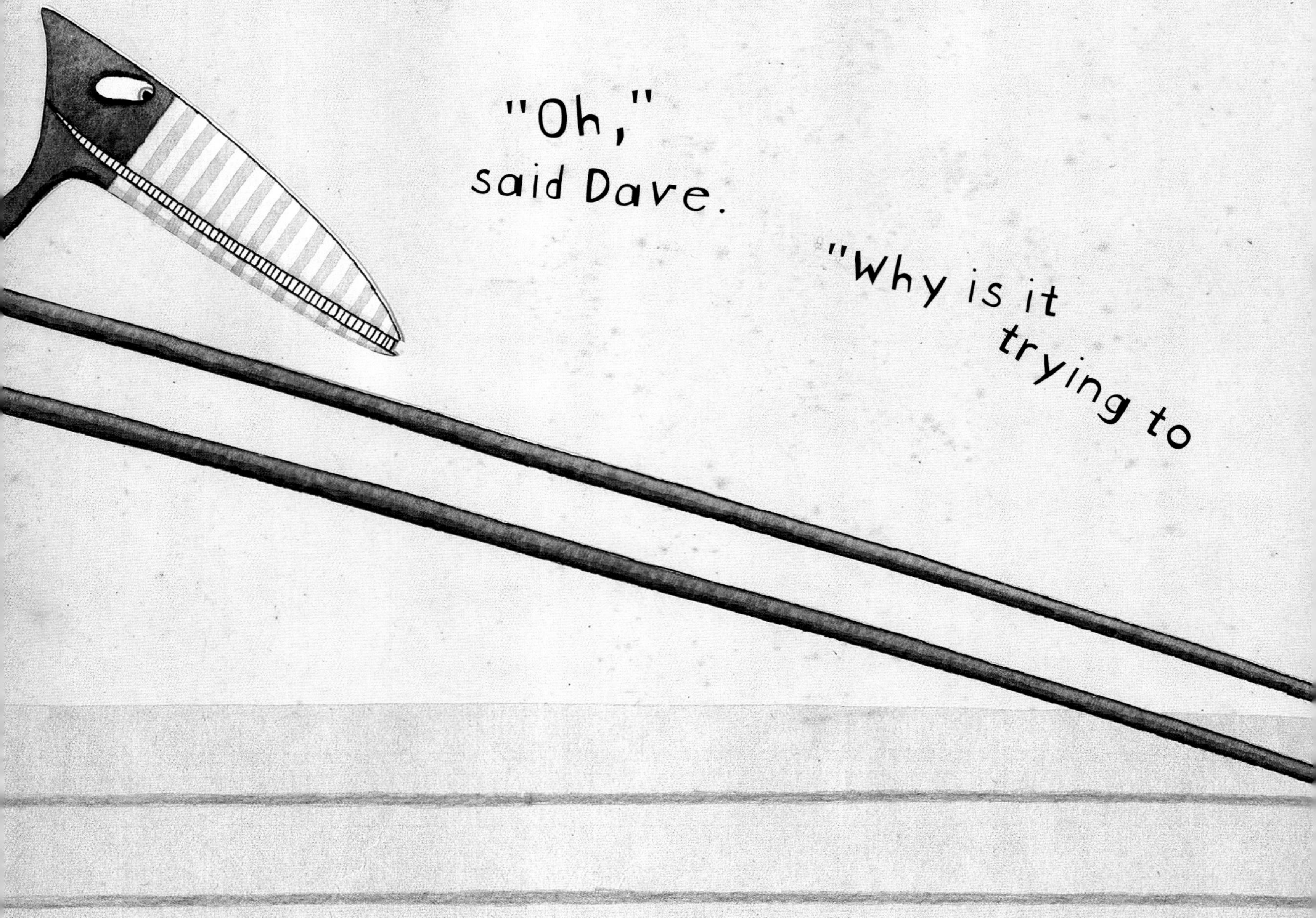

"Oh,"
said Dave.

"Why is it
trying to

"Deinocheirus
don't tickle, Dave,"
Dad laughed,
"it's just your
imagination."

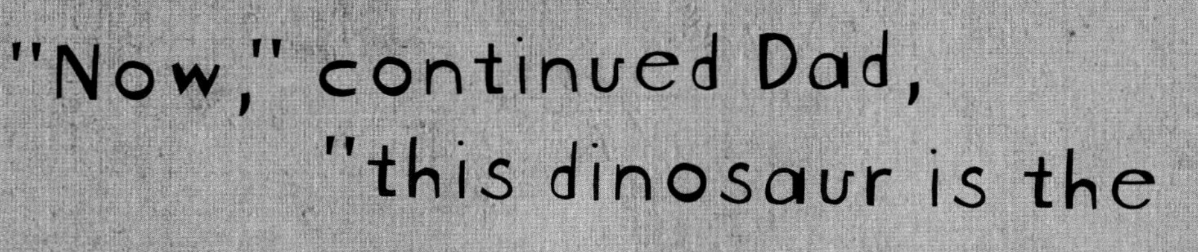

"Now," continued Dad,
"this dinosaur is the
Allosaurus.
It has
long,
sharp
teeth."

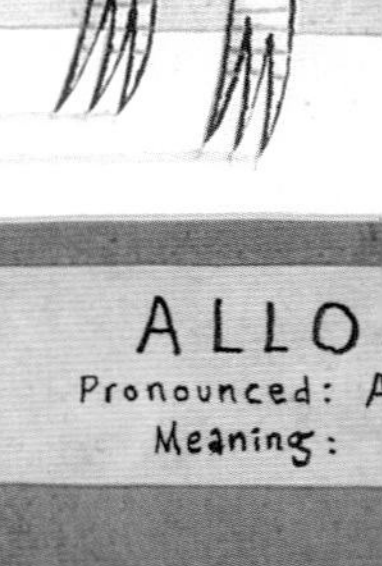

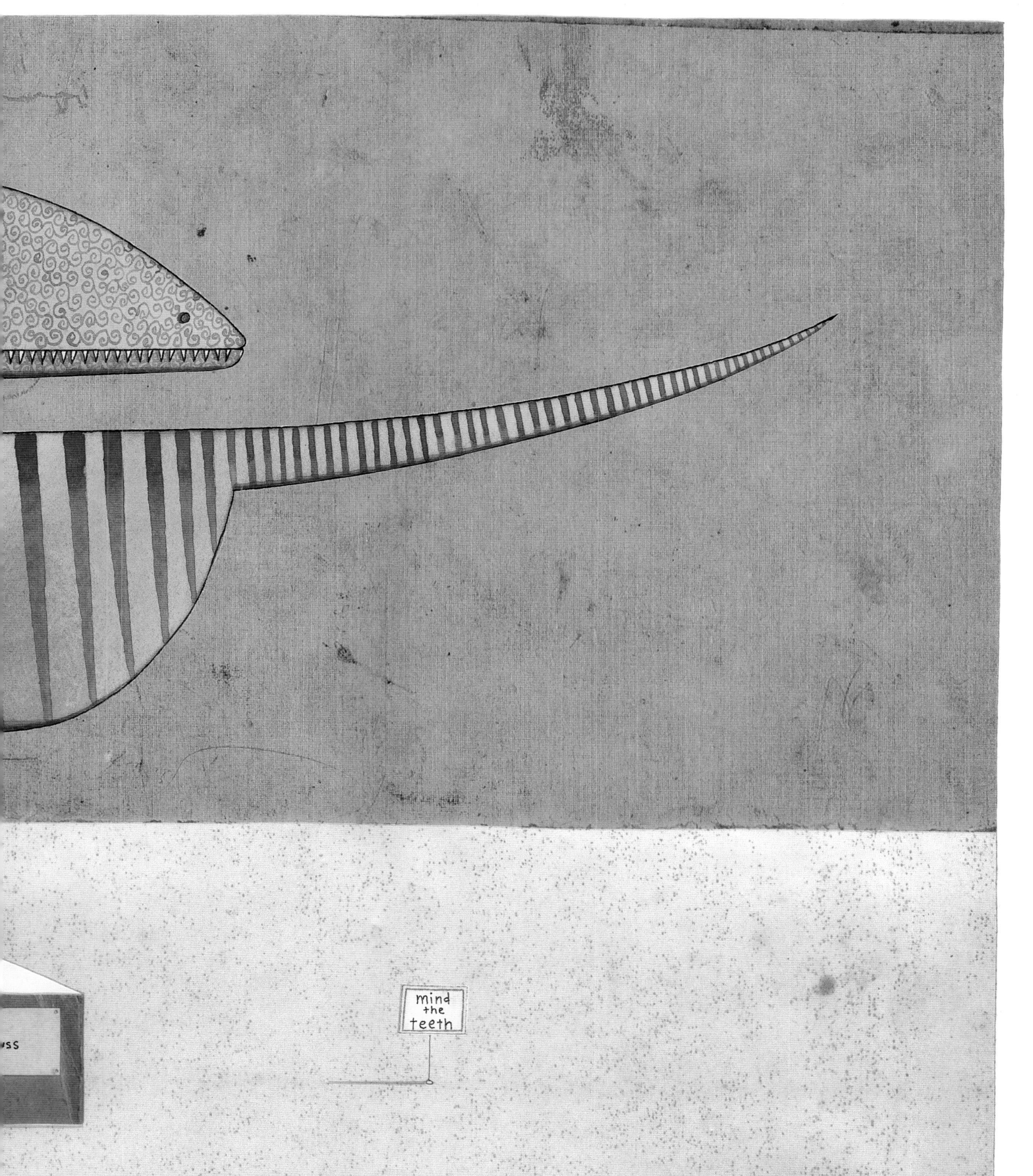
mind
the
teeth

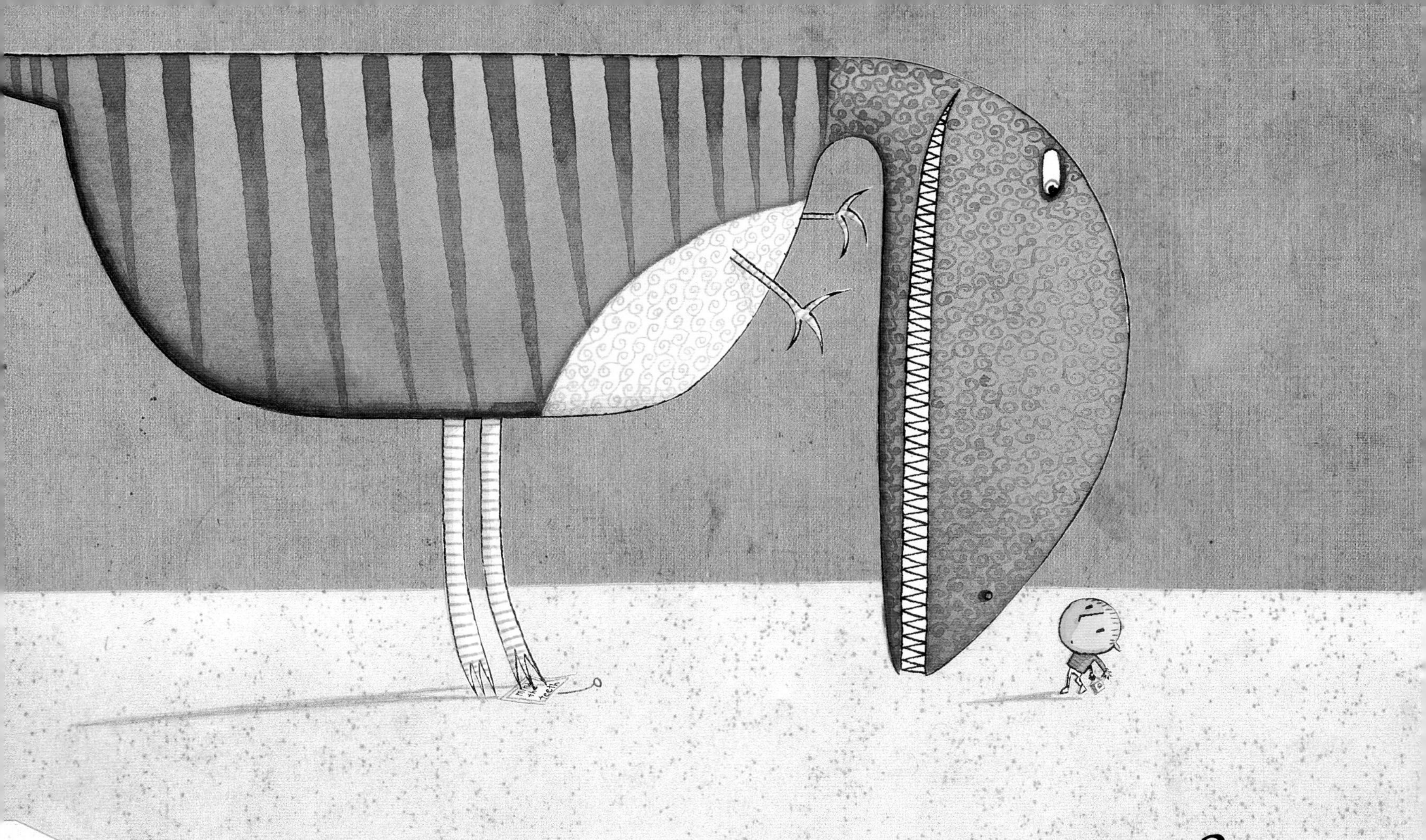

"Oh," said Dave.
"Why is it grinning
at me, Dad?"

"Allosaurus
don't grin, Dave,"
smiled Dad,
"it's just your
imagination."

Dad moved on to the next dinosaur.

"Ah! You see this one with the very long neck, Dave,

that's a Diplodocus."

"Oh," said Dave. "Why is it. .

...trying to eat my burger?"
"Diplodocus
don't eat burgers, Dave,"
explained Dad,
"they're herbivores.
It's just your
imagination."

"And finally, son,
here we have the

Tyrannosaurus Rex,

one of the largest
meat-eating
dinosaurs
that
ever
lived."

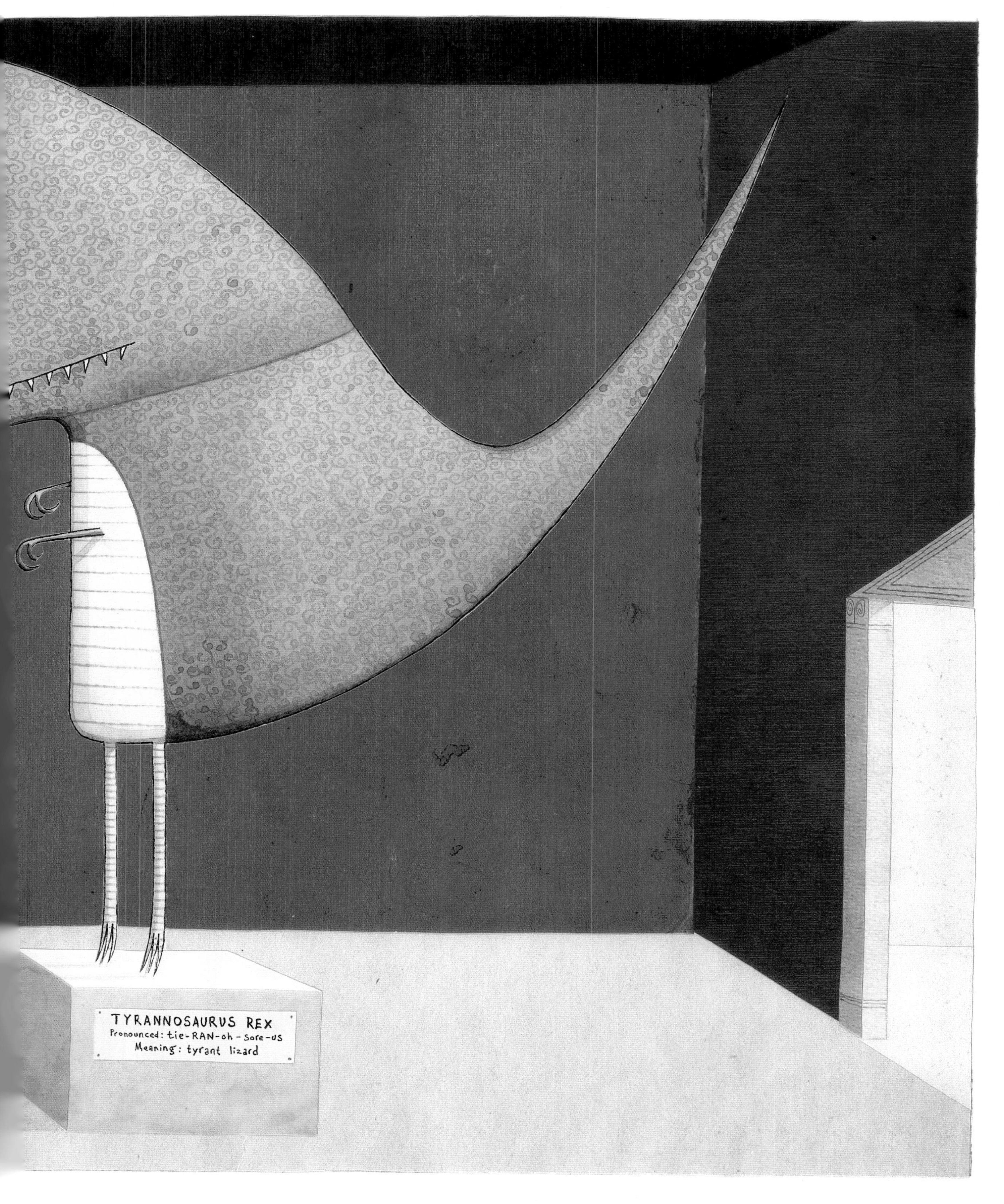
TYRANNOSAURUS REX
Pronounced: tie-RAN-oh-sore-us
Meaning: tyrant lizard

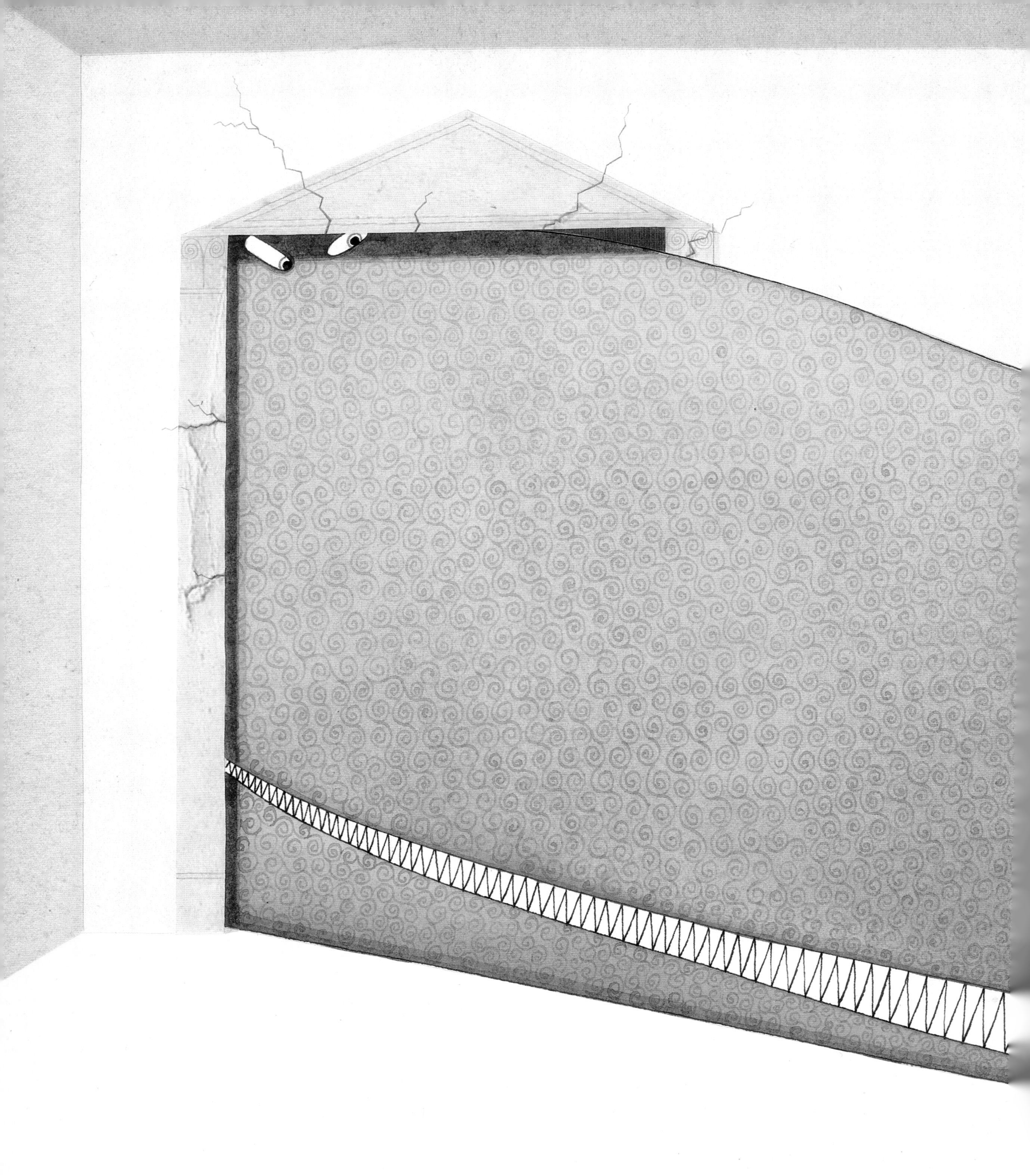

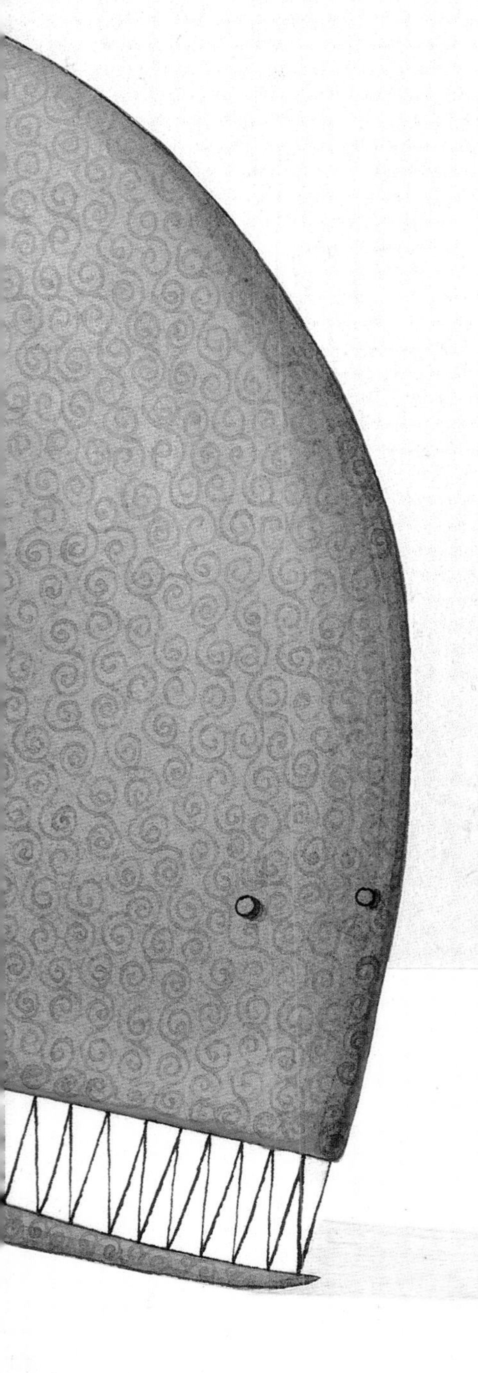

"OH!!"

said Dave.

"So you see, Dave," said Dad,
"the dinosaurs
are indeed
dead."

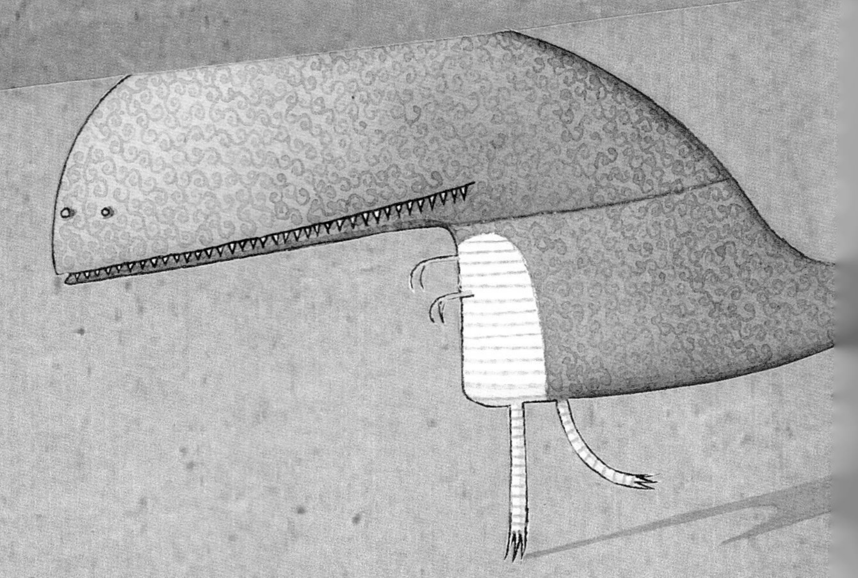

"Then why is that one

following us, Dad?"

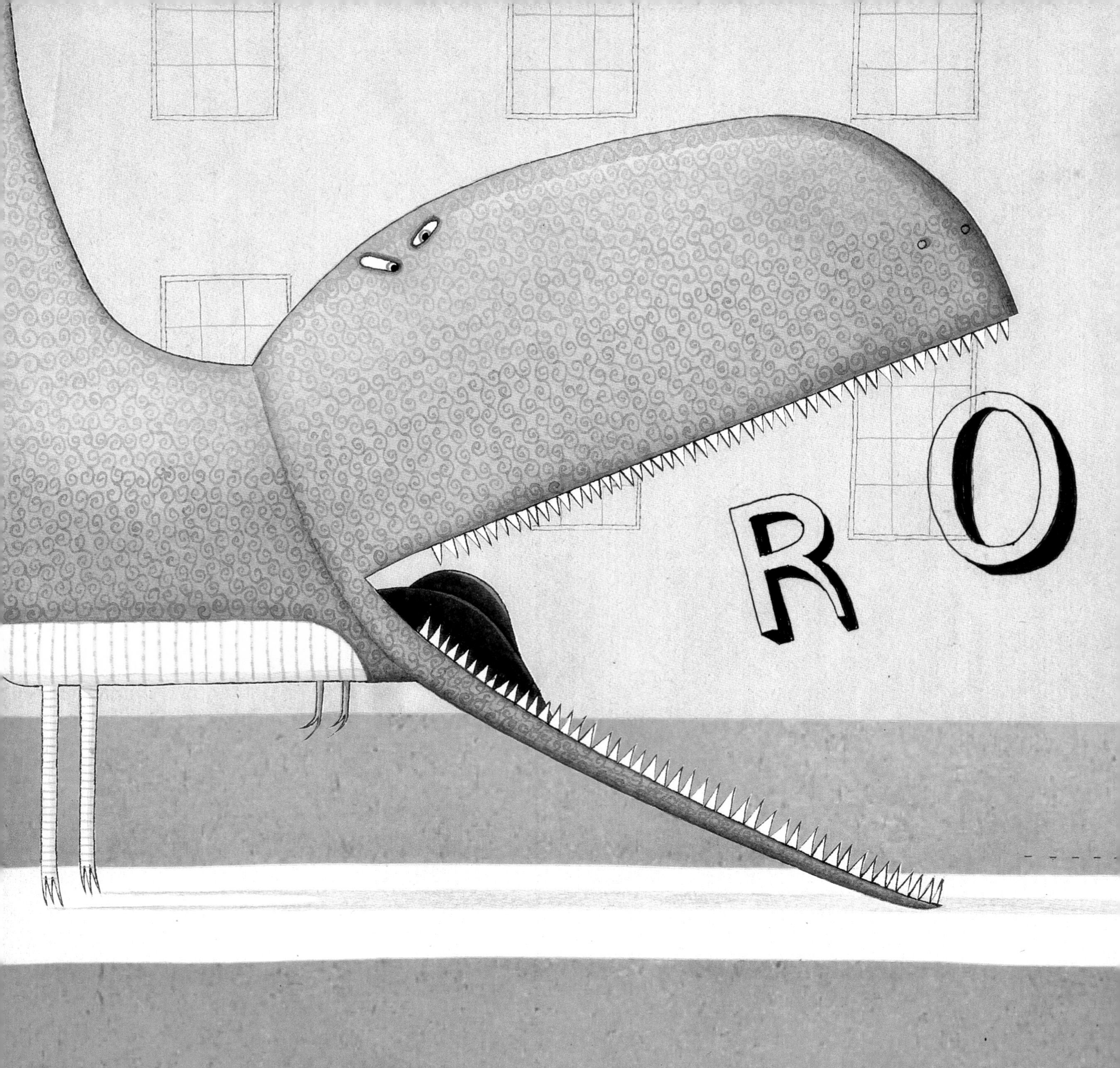
R O

AR!!

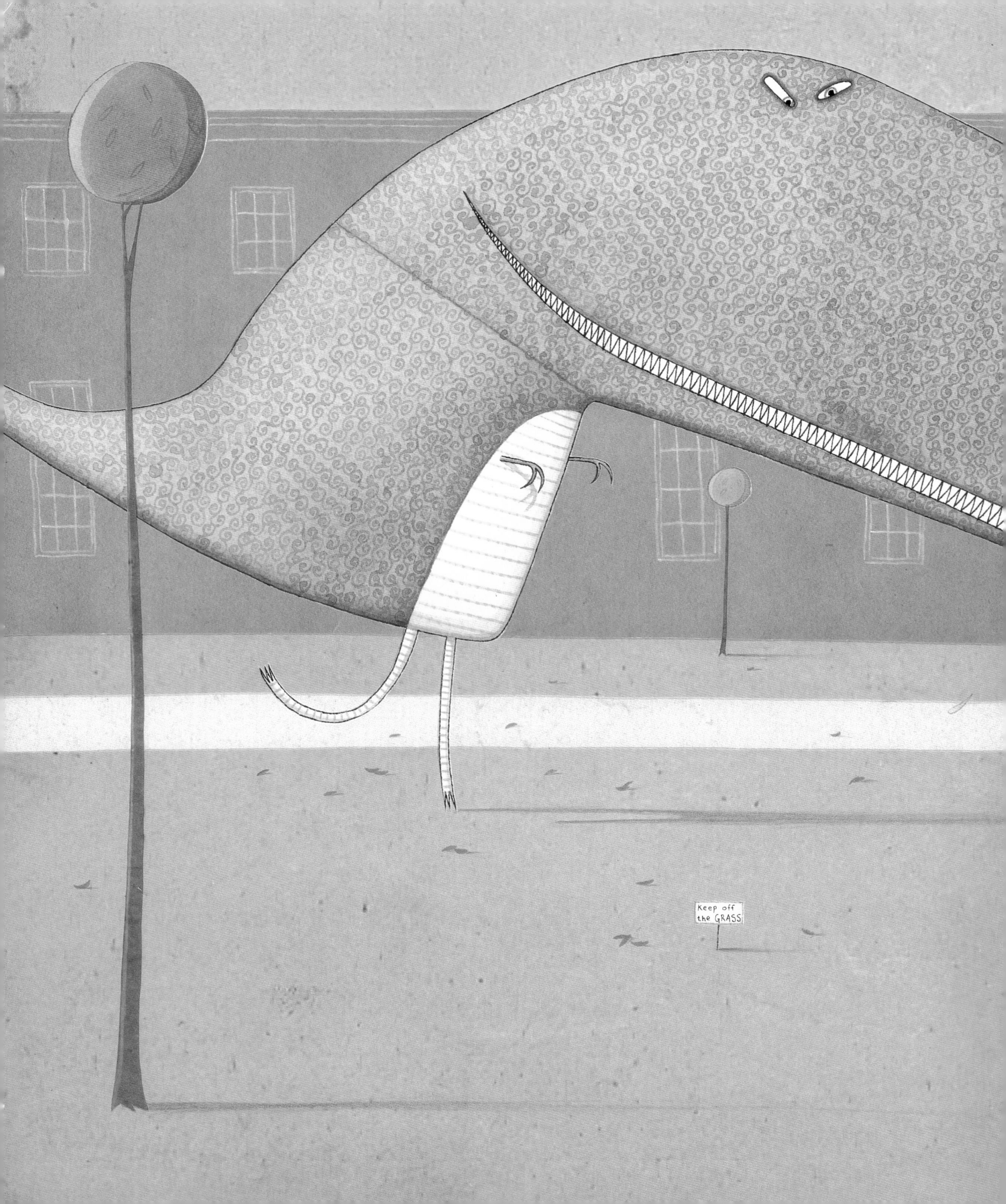
Keep off
the GRASS

"Oh! You're right, Dave," said Dad. "That dinosaur's not dead."

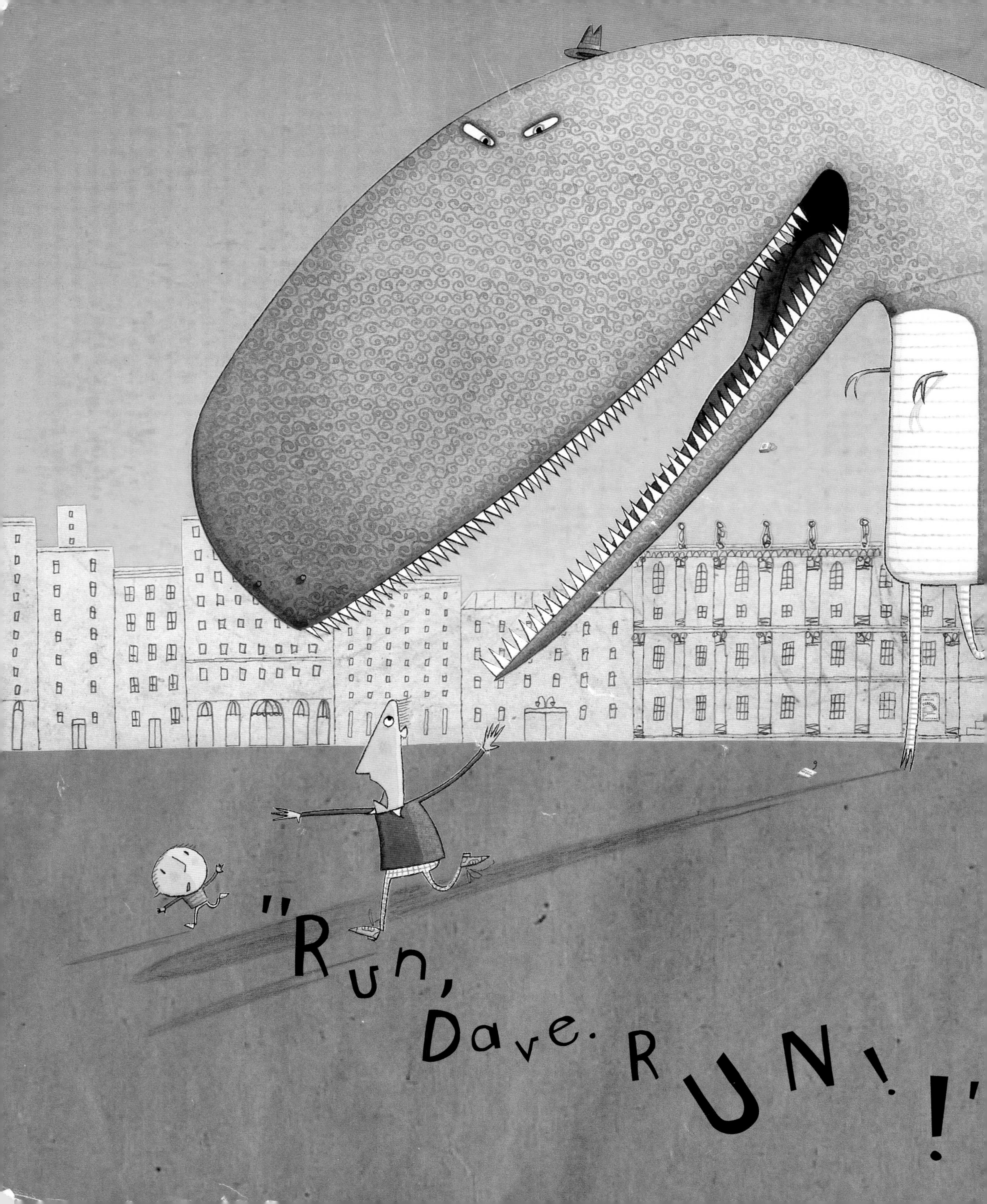
"Run, Dave. RUN!!"